CAVE DADA PICKY EATER

BRANDON REESE

chronicle books · san francisco

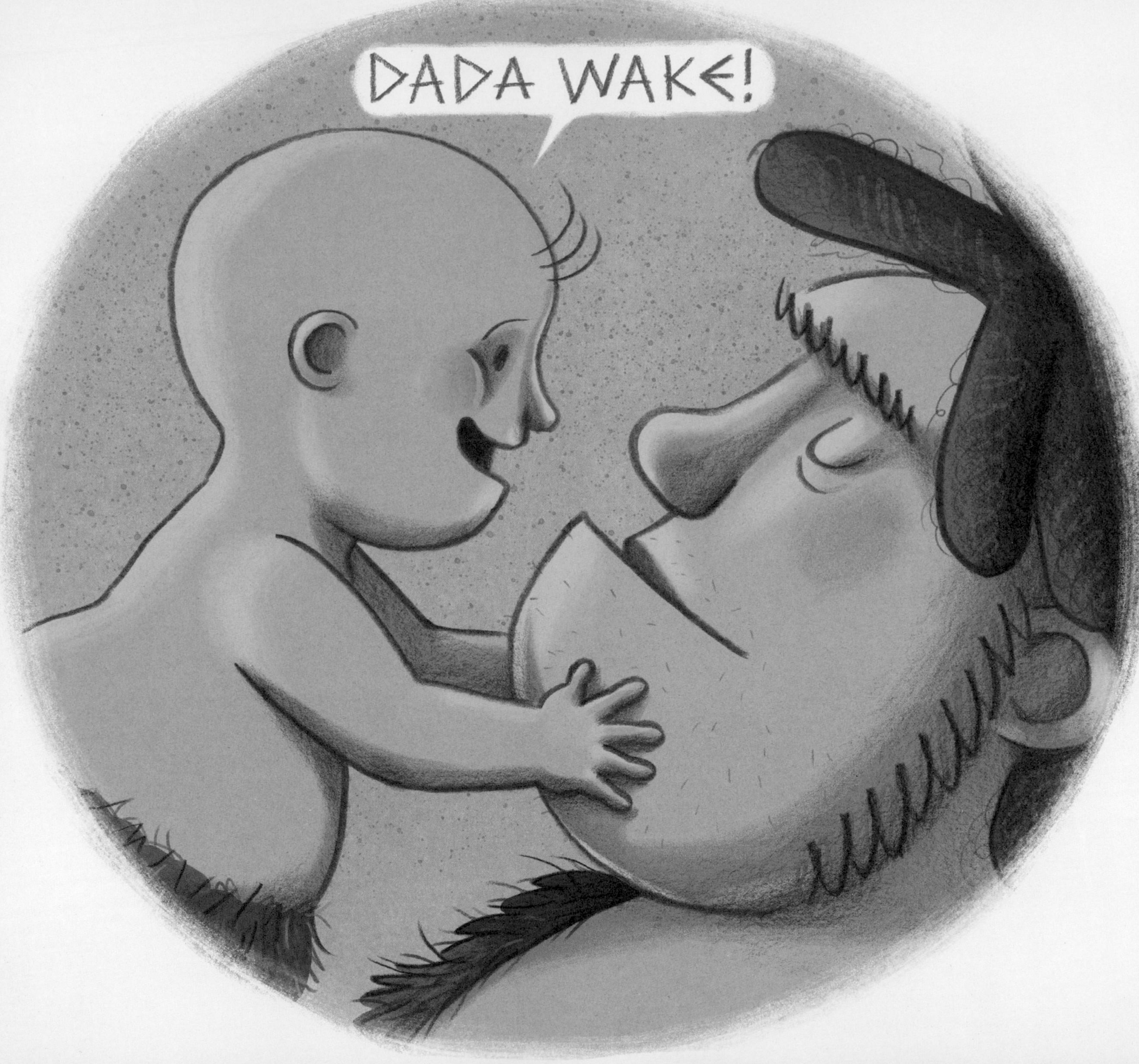
DADA WAKE!

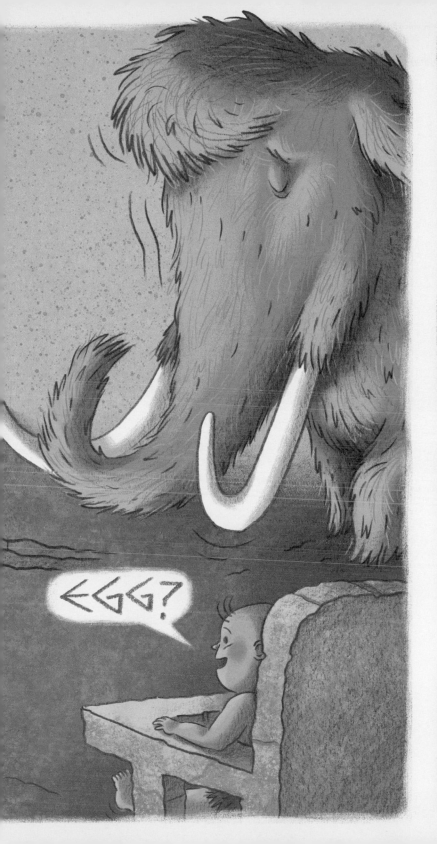

BABA, PLEASE NO CRY.
DADA NO WANT HUNT GATHER.
DADA DAY OFF... DADA WANT RELAX.

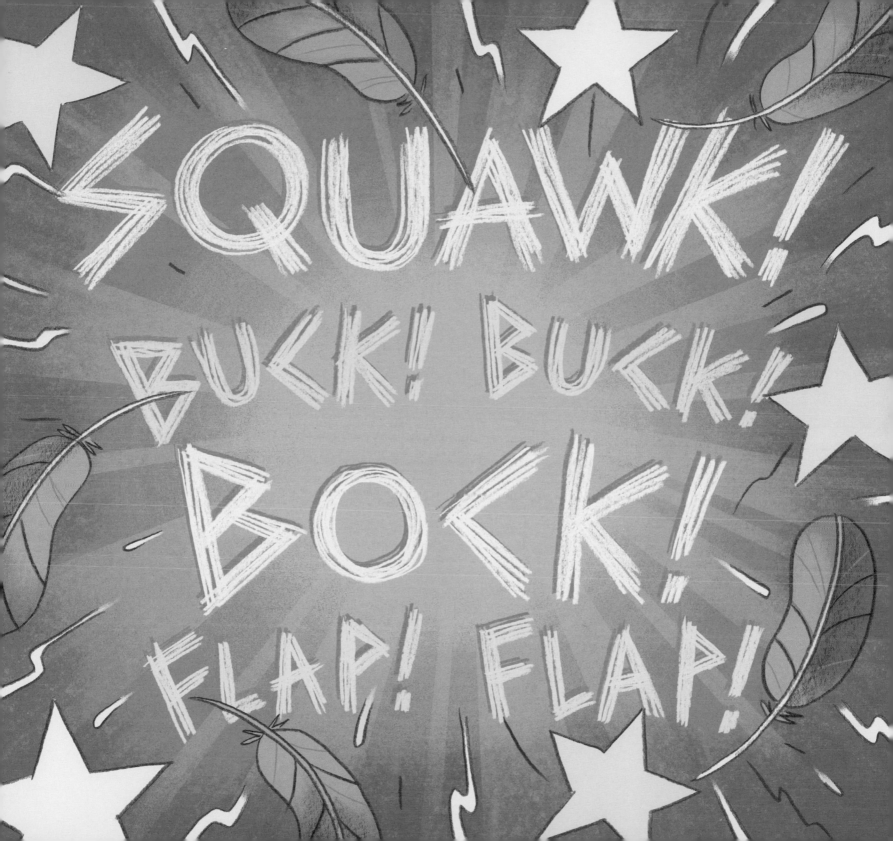

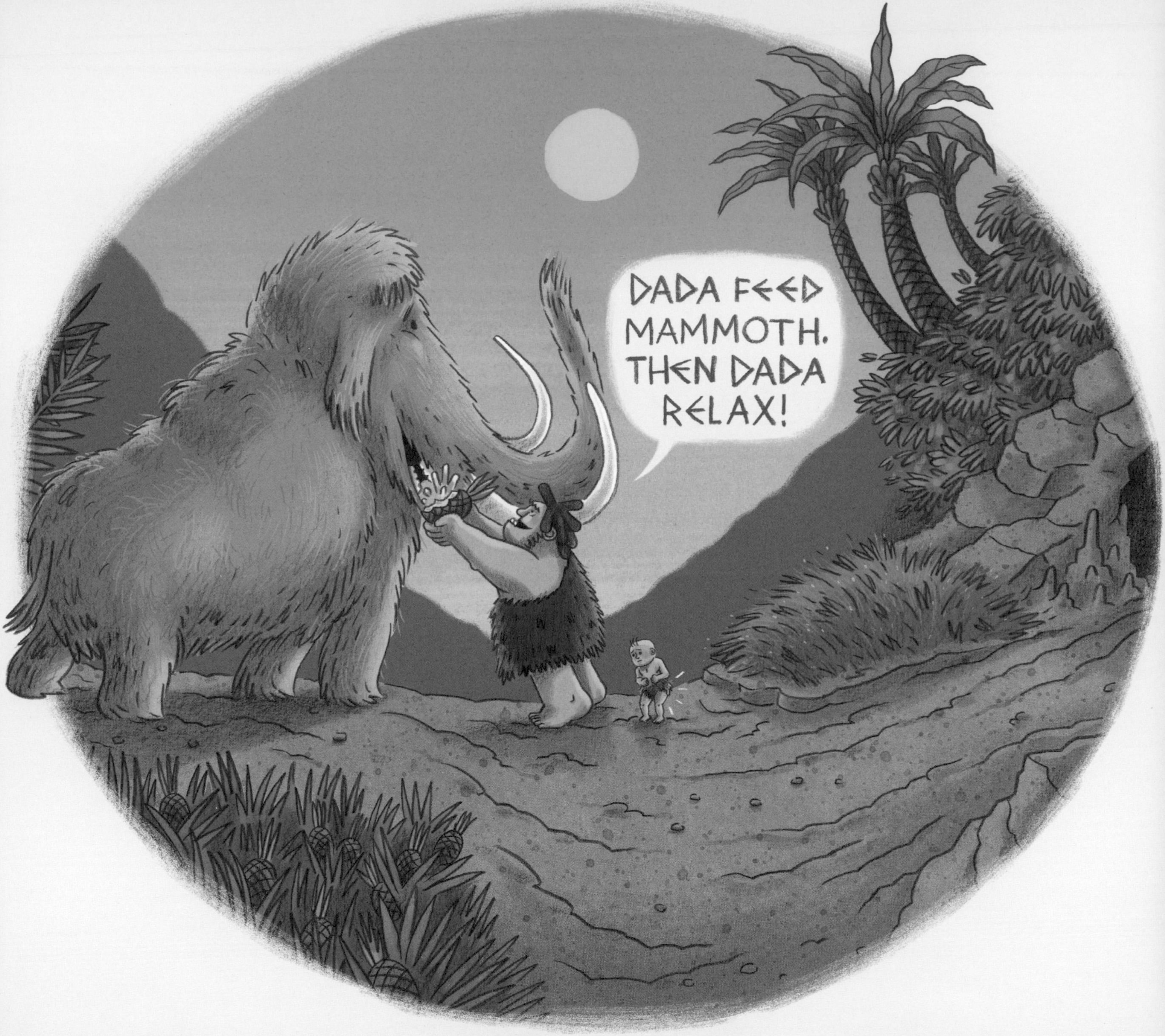
DADA FEED MAMMOTH. THEN DADA RELAX!

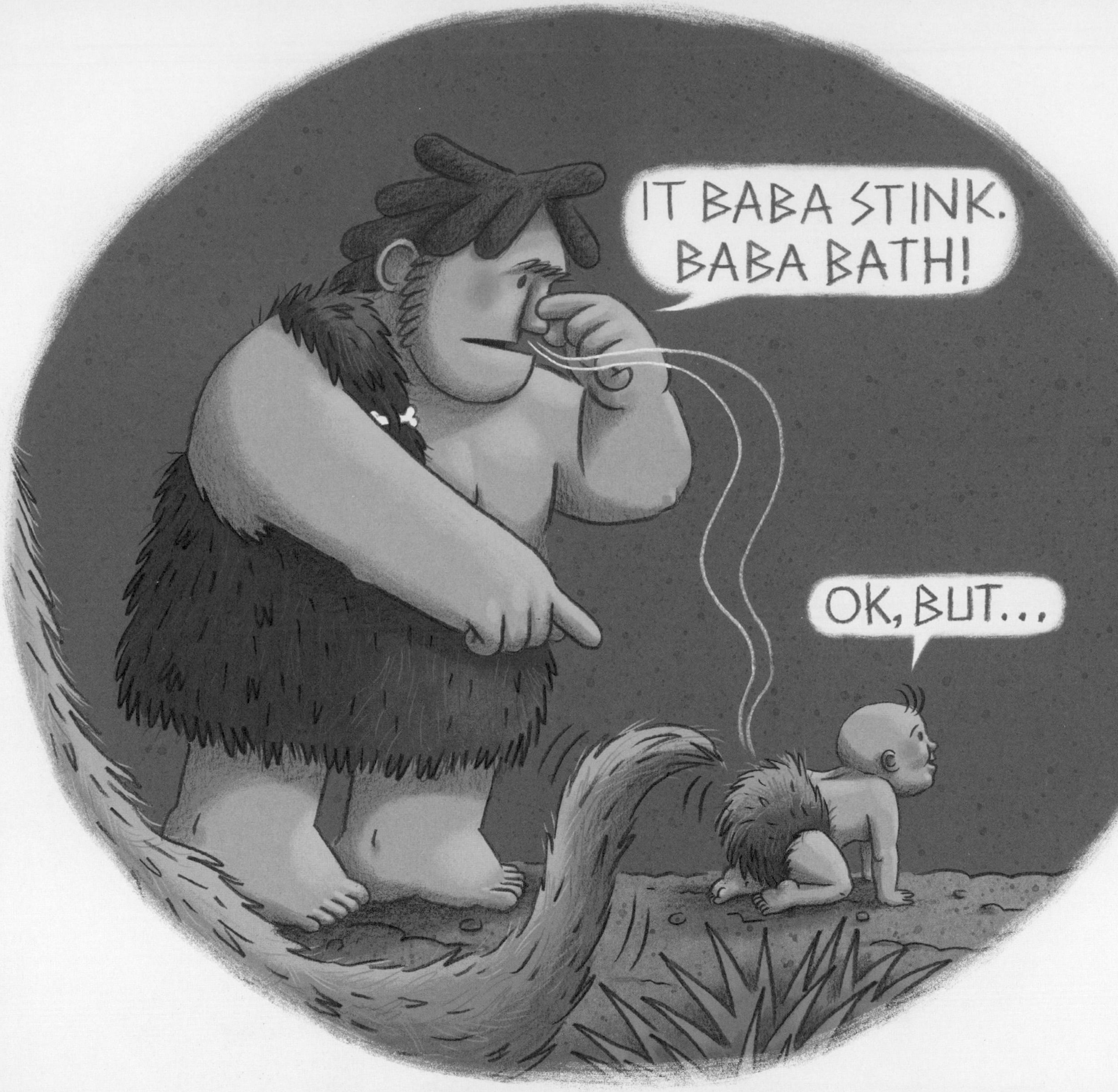
IT BABA STINK.
BABA BATH!
OK, BUT...

FOR JB...MY BEST FRIEND
SINCE THE STONE AGE.

Library of Congress Cataloging-in-Publication
Data available.

ISBN 978-1-4521-7995-7

Manufactured in China.

MIX
Paper from
responsible sources
FSC™ C008047

Design by Jay Marvel.
Typeset in Gaegu.

The illustrations in this book were rendered in
colored pencil, gouache, and Adobe Photoshop.

10 9 8 7 6 5 4 3 2 1

Chronicle Books LLC
680 Second Street
San Francisco, California 94107

Chronicle Books—we see things differently. Become
part of our community at www.chroniclekids.com.